Kk   Ll   Mm

Nn   Oo

Pp   Qq   Rr

Ss   Tt   Uu

Vv   Ww

Xx   Yy   Zz

To My Friends at The Children's Place: The CiCi & Ace adventures continue thanks to the leadership of your wonderful team. Thank you for caring about children and bringing fun and the joy of learning into their lives.

To Douglas, Jared, Cameron and Jazz: You are the inspiration for all of CiCi and Ace's adventures. Thank you for listening to my new stories and music. It's such a joy to see you dancing around, singing my songs, quoting my characters, and acting out their adventures making them your own.

To Mom and Dad: Thank you for always making learning fun. From car games we played to hands-on science projects we dreamed up, you made education a way of life. Dad, thanks for teaching me so many life lessons you can't find in books. Mom, your 35 years of teaching school and your love for educating our next generation made a lasting impression, and I'm trying to carry on where you left off. I guess you never did leave off – you're still at it! But, mostly thank you for teaching me to believe in myself, and for even believing in me when I wasn't quite ready to do it for myself.

To Patricia: You are my all-time favorite teacher who encouraged my love of reading and creative writing through your magic in the classroom. Thank you for sharing your creative spark through years of support and friendship. Can you believe you are still grading my papers? These days, we're calling it proofing.

To Frank: Thank you for working with me to make the music and characters I hear in my head just right for my stories and the children who hear them. Your talent is so appreciated.

To Laurie: You were my first real friend in elementary school, and you are still one of my closest friends. Remember all the notes I wrote telling you how much your friendship means -- they're still true.

To Karin and Zenon: Thanks for bringing my ideas and vision to life in a way that truly entertains and delights children and adults.

I Love You All, Rainey

Produced Exclusively for
The Children's Place
by DreamDog Press
3686 King Street, Suite 160
Alexandria, VA 22302

Order online @ **www.childrensplace.com**

Copyright © 2004 The Children's Place
Created and Written by Rainey (Lorraine Lee Friedman)
Illustrated by Karin Huggens
Graphic Design and Type Treatment by Zenon Slawinski

Cataloging-in-Publication Data
Rainey (aka Friedman, Lorraine Lee.)
School is Cool! by Rainey; illustrated by Karin Huggens – 1st ed.
p.cm.
SUMMARY: At school, CiCi and Ace learn a very important lesson – to believe in themselves. This book shows how a positive attitude and the power of a child's confidence can turn school into a great adventure. Included is a Sing-Along Music CD with original songs, a Note for Families about building self-esteem, and a Family Art Activity.

ISBN: 0-9666199-8-7
1. Discovery and learning – Juvenile Fiction. 2. Brother and sister adventure -- Juvenile Fiction
3. Self-esteem and skill building at school –Juvenile Fiction. 4. First day of school – Juvenile Fiction.
1. Huggens, Karin II.Title

SCHOOL IS COOL!

by Rainey

Illustrated by
Karin Huggens

I remember CiCi's first day at school.
I said, "You'll have a great time –
SCHOOL IS COOL!"

Dad hugged us good-bye,
then gave us one big **SQUEEZE** more
and said, "I love you guys" and
headed out the door.

Mom walked to the corner with both of us.
We met other kids waiting for the bus.

Their moms were smoothing hair and wiping faces,
checking their backpacks and lunch box cases.

Mom's whole face lit up with a smile
and she said, "CiCi, honey, I love your style."
My sister was in Princess gear from head to toes,
decked out in pink and **purple**, with big new bows.

Her backpack was purple with a pink crown.
Since we bought it, she'd hardly put it down.
We got a smooch from Mom and a "You'll do great."
Then we piled on the bus, not wanting to be late.

CiCi sat real close to me for the whole ride.
I wondered what she was feeling inside.

She smiled and said, "I'm so excited, Ace.
But what if I get lost? It's such a big place."

"CiCi, you stay with your teacher and class all day even at lunch time or when you go outside to play.

But, if you ever need me, you just call. I'll hear you; my class is right down the hall."

As we walked into school,
she grabbed my hand real tight.
In my big brother voice, I said, "It'll be all right."

"But," she asked,
"what if I don't know anyone?"
"Hey," I answered, "that's part of the fun.
School is the place to meet new friends.
It's an adventure that never ends."

Inside, she found a cubby with her name,
hung up her pack, and said, "Let's play a game."

She picked the table with puzzles and blocks,
then found a hand puppet made from socks.

I said good-bye and gave her ponytail a tug.
She followed me to the door for one more hug.

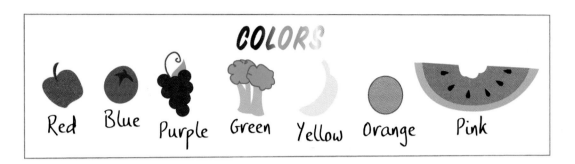

"Have fun," I called as she ran to the dress-up box
and waved good-bye with two hand puppet socks.

Her room was so colorful, filled with fun things to do.
I knew she'd have good stories
by the time school was through.

Then it was my turn to buzz down the hall,
and I made it to my desk before roll call.

My new teacher smiled and told us his name.
And we all played a "Get-To-Know-You" game.

He said tomorrow we would introduce ourselves
with banners he would hang by our classroom shelves.
We could draw on them, paint them, or use glitter or glue.
It was totally our choice what we wanted to do.
He asked us to tell a summer memory,
and I smiled and thought about Za-ru-pee.

I had music, science and gym that day
but just kept thinking about what I would say.

Should I tell my class about drinking blue tea?

I picked up CiCi in her classroom after school.
She met me with a smile, "You're right, SCHOOL IS COOL!"
On the bus, she talked about sharing and circle time
and how she raised her hand and knew how to rhyme.

"Cat rhymes with hat!"

I heard a story about her new best friend, Mae,
whom she invited over to our house to play.
But, the whole time she talked quite excitedly,

I pictured all those eyes looking at me.

Mom met us at the door with after-school snacks,
hugged us, and kissed us, then grabbed our backpacks.
"So...tell me all about your first day."
CiCi started talking as I walked away.

"Hey Ace," Mom called, "I want to hear about your day, too."
"Nothing much to tell, Mom – I've got homework to do."
CiCi said, "When I finish, I want to help, too."
So we went to my room and she colored while I drew.

Then, CiCi said something really wise
when I told her I was scared of all those eyes.

"You can do it if you try.
Just look your classmates in the eye.
Say your speech clear and loud.
You'll make yourself really proud."

I heard her words echo in my head
even when I tried to go to bed.

You can do it if you try.
You'll make yourself really proud.

The next day, CiCi patted me on the back
and said, "You can do it Ace, just stay on track."

She walked into her room and hugged her friend Mae.
And I thought, "What a change in just one day."

In my class we took turns, one by one.
Hearing my friends' stories was lots of fun.
When it was my turn, I heard the words CiCi said
and felt my face grow kind of red.

I started with the picture of my family,
the one where CiCi is sitting on my knee.
I went on to tell them how much I liked sports
and animals and dinosaurs of all sorts.

When I told my favorite summer memory,
I felt every eye in the classroom on me.
My teacher asked about my green friend
and that's when my shyness came to an end.

I told the class about our MAGIC ride
and the adventures we all have inside.
Then, I told them about Za-ru-pee
and the dance he taught CiCi and me.

I know that afternoon my face was beaming
when CiCi saw me and started screaming,

"You did it! You did it! I knew you could.
You told your story and told it good."

"CiCi, they were all dancing, too!
What you said was really true.
Believing in yourself is the most important tool,
one you definitely need to succeed in school."

SCHOOL BUS

Then I added, "For a little sister, you're really cool."
"You are, too," she smiled and said, "so is school!"

Confidence...School Success...and Our Children

Children's self-esteem and confidence can determine not only their success in school, but how much they enjoy learning and how well they adapt socially. How do we share the gift of self-confidence with our children? How do we make them see that in order to do well, they must first believe in themselves?

Self-confidence comes from both the messages our children hear about themselves and the messages they create for themselves. Here are some tools we can use to help build self-esteem and confidence in our children:

- **Praise your children.** Find a way to praise your children every single day and do so with **specifics**. Even when they don't do something perfectly or the way you wanted them to, praise their efforts. Comments like "Good job coloring that picture -- I love the way you drew purple hair!" or "That puzzle looked like a tough one, but you kept trying -- I'm really proud of you!" build a child's self-esteem.
- **Have realistic expectations.** Give your children the opportunity to do things in their own ways. It doesn't matter how good they are at something. It's more important that they are trying and doing their best. Remember that they are gaining life experiences and may not have the developmental skills to do certain tasks. Allow them to just be kids.
- **Focus on strengths not weaknesses.** Children can be sensitive to criticism and negative messages. Provide correction gently while pointing out their strengths.
- **Allow for and encourage their uniqueness.** Avoid comparing siblings or comparing your child to a playmate. Instead, compliment them on what makes them special and encourage the unique child that they are to shine through.
- **Reassure your children that you love them.** Your children must believe that your love is unconditional. There are countless ways to show your children that you love them: through snuggles, hugs, kisses, playing with them, talking and listening to them. Remember to say, "I love you" every single day. Children will feel loved and worthy of love when they hear this message.
- **Create an environment of mutual trust through choice.** You should trust your children to do the right thing, and create trust by communicating your love for them. Put trust into action by allowing them to make choices. This can be as simple as what to wear to school, what they want for lunch, or how to resolve a conflict with a friend, but it sends the message, "I believe in you and trust you."
- **Listen to what is happening in your children's lives.** Stay involved. Ask questions. Show you care by being an active participant in their lives. Let your children know how important they are by really listening and trying to understand what they have to say.
- **Allow for mistakes.** Giving your children the freedom to tackle new situations and challenges is a true self-esteem builder. Be there if they need you for support and encouragement, but allow them to work through new, and sometimes fearful, situations. This will help them understand that they can handle new challenges.
- **Encourage self-pride.** It is important that our children not only hear, "I'm so proud of you," but also that they can send that message to themselves. Teaching our children to be proud of themselves is a self-esteem building skill that they can learn.
- **Be a positive role model.** Children model their behaviors based on what they see and experience. Try to exhibit the positive values, upbeat outlook, and character that you want your children to reflect.

By building your child's self-esteem, you are giving them the inner strength to handle life's ups and downs, get along with others, and keep trying even if they don't get something right the first time. You are giving them the skills to succeed, not only in school -- but also in life!

Interactive Family Art Activity
Create a "Banner of ME!"

A great hands-on way to build self-esteem is through family art projects. Every "artist" will bring his or her own creative ideas and style to the project. Give your children the chance to make their own choices and to be proud of the end product that they create. Here's an awesome way to have fun and let your children focus on their own unique sense of self...help them create a "Banner of Me!"

These steps are just meant as a guide. Use them as a starting point and add your own creative touches to make a very special banner. You can visit us at childrensplace.com for more ideas.

You will need:
- A long sheet of paper, or a few poster boards taped together
- Markers, crayons, paints, glitter – whatever you want to use to decorate your banner
- Pictures of family, friends, and pets
- Magazine cut outs of favorite things
- Glue or tape

Step 1 - Give it a Fun Title
At the top of your paper, think of a title for your banner. It can say "Banner of Me!" like the one Ace made, or "All About Me!" or even "Watch Out, Here I Come!" Think of your own fun title or use one of these.

Step 2 - Choose Topics that Tell About You
Pick your topics or the categories that you will use to highlight things that make you unique. You might want to include some of Ace's topics: my family, my favorite things, my favorite memory. Or, you can come up with your own topics: favorite foods, favorite fashions, my friends, animals I like, what I want to be when I grow up, words that describe me, etc.

Step 3 - Create a Mixed Media Message
Now, tell your story about Unique Wonderful You using all kinds of artistic techniques. As the story says:

You can draw on them, paint them or use glitter or glue. It is totally your choice what you want to do!

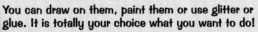

You can paint some of your topics, cut some out of magazines and paste them on, glitter your favorite words, and use fabrics to show your favorite styles or colors. There's no limit to what you can create. Remember, it's totally your choice. Exercise your options and just have fun.

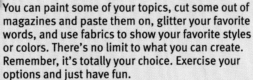

Step 4 - Tell Your Tale
Now, do what Ace did – display your "Banner of Me" and explain all about you. Make up stories or songs to tell all about One-of-a-Kind You. You can even ask family members to help act out parts of your banner. And, don't forget to bow or curtsey at the end of your show.

Now tell your story, clear and loud.
You'll make yourself really proud!

School is Cool!

Woke up early in the morning, first day of school,
I jumped out of bed and said, "Oh cool!"
I brushed my teeth and washed my face,
Put on new clothes at a lightning pace.

I'm going – going back to school.
See my old friends; hope the adventure never ends.
School is cool!

Down to breakfast with my whole family:
There's Mom, Dad, Baby, CiCi and Me.
And, Mom is fixin' somethin' for our lunch.
She is gonna miss us – I've got a hunch.

But, we're going – going back to school.
Vacation was fun, but now it's done.
School is cool!

Grab your lunch box and your pack.
It'll be late before we're back.
Now, hop on the bus, for just a quick ride.
"Look at all the kids inside."

We're going – going back to school.
You can sing along. It's an easy song.
School is cool!

CiCi is nervous. "It's my very first day."
I tell her about all the games she'll play.
Meetin' new friends, having a blast,
Learnin' new stuff…the day's over too fast.

That's the way – the way it is at school.
It's all up to you. You know what to do.
School is cool!

The very first day seemed to fly.
Picked my little sister up and saw the twinkle in her eye.
She said, "You're right. It was great.
More tomorrow; I can hardly wait.

I love it! I love it here at school!
I met new friends; hope the adventure never ends.
School is cool!"

You'll love it – you're gonna love your school.
You'll meet new friends; the adventure never ends.
School is cool!

Sha-na-na-na. Sha-na-na-na-na-na.
Sha-na-na-na. Sha-na-na-na-na-na.
Sha-na-na-na. Sha-na-na-na-na-na.
School is Cool!

Be Who You Are!

Going to school is really cool.
You learn somethin' new each day.
And you meet lots of friends
as you learn and play.

But, there's one thing that I know
that I've learned along the way.
And I would like to share it
with you here today:

You gotta be who you are.
Jump for a star.
Believe in you
and your dreams come true.
Just be who you are.

There's a lot to learn in school
that's not in any book,
like how to get along
or deal with a mad look.

There's so much more to school
than learning ABC's,
or how to count your numbers
or say thanks and please.

You gotta be who you are.
Jump for a star.
Try anything
and let your heart sing.
Just be who you are.

My sister is a Princess,
that's what she likes to play,
and she even came to school
and dressed up that way.

And, when the bully laughed,
and said, "Oh, look at you."
CiCi smiled back and said,
"You can be a Princess, too."

You gotta be who you are.
Jump for a star.
Have your own style
and the world will smile.
Just be who you are.

Some kids at school act really tough.
Some others, they act shy.
But I just have to smile
and look them in the eye.

'Cause I know that I can do
any thing that I try to.
I believe in myself
through and through.